BUTT OUT!

HEATH McKENZIE

A Scholastic Press book from Scholastic Australia

FOR AVA & OSCAR–

butts out whenever and wherever possible!

Scholastic Press
An imprint of Scholastic Australia Pty Limited (ABN 11 000 614 577)
PO Box 579 Gosford NSW 2250
www.scholastic.com.au

Part of the Scholastic Group
Sydney · Auckland · New York · Toronto · London · Mexico City
· New Delhi · Hong Kong · Buenos Aires · Puerto Rico

First published by Scholastic Australia in 2018.
This edition published in 2024.

A catalogue record for this book is available from the National Library of Australia

ISBN: 978-1-76152-583-4

Typeset in Agnes by Hand and Lovage.

Printed in China by RR Donnelley.
Scholastic Australia's policy, in association with RR Donnelley, is to use papers that are renewable and efficiently with wood from responsibly managed sources, so as to minimise its environmental footprint.

10 9 8 7 6 5 4 3 2 1 24 25 26 27 28 / 2

TODAY FEELS LIKE A

GOOD DAY

TO BE . . .

PANTS
FREE!

Good HEAVENS!
Your BOTTOM is out!

SUN'S OUT,

BUNS

OUT!

Excuse me, I do believe
you've forgotten your PANTS!

I DO BELIEVE
I **NEVER** PUT ANY
ON!

For the good of the children!
PLEASE put your BUTT away!

AND **MISS**
THIS SUMMER BREEZE
BETWEEN MY
CHEEKS?

But . . .
but . . .
but . . .

YES!

YES, IT IS!

Hey, cut it OUT!

MORE LIKE,

BUTT

IT OUT.

Oi, BUDDY! Do us all a favour!
COVER ya BUTT!!!

I WOULD . . .

BUT I

WON'T!

BUTT IN NOT OUT!!!
LESS CHEEK! MORE CHINO!
SLIP! SLOP! SLACKS!

RIGHT!

There is a time and a place for many things but now is NOT the time or place for bare bottoms, so can you PLEASE . . .

JUST PUT SOME

PANTS ON!

FINE.

UTT
IN
NO

PANTS ARE ON!

NOW YOU CAN

ALL . . .

BUTT OUT!